Dear Parent:
Your child's love of reading starts here!

Every child learns to read in a different way and at his or her own speed. Some go back and forth between reading levels and read favorite books again and again. Others read through each level in order. You can help your young reader improve and become more confident by encouraging his or her own interests and abilities. From books your child reads with you to the first books he or she reads alone, there are I Can Read Books for every stage of reading:

SHARED READING
Basic language, word repetition, and whimsical illustrations, ideal for sharing with your emergent reader

BEGINNING READING
Short sentences, familiar words, and simple concepts for children eager to read on their own

READING WITH HELP
Engaging stories, longer sentences, and language play for developing readers

READING ALONE
Complex plots, challenging vocabulary, and high-interest topics for the independent reader

ADVANCED READING
Short paragraphs, chapters, and exciting themes for the perfect bridge to chapter books

I Can Read Books have introduced children to the joy of reading since 1957. Featuring award-winning authors and illustrators and a fabulous cast of beloved characters, I Can Read Books set the standard for beginning readers.

A lifetime of discovery begins with the magical words "I Can Read!"

*Visit www.icanread.com for information
on enriching your child's reading experience.*

To Luke (who really loves Spike)
—K.G.

To everyone who loves spring,
despite allergies ☺
—O.V.

I Can Read Book® is a trademark of HarperCollins Publishers.

Duck, Duck, Dinosaur: Spring Smiles
Copyright © 2019 by HarperCollins Publishers.
www.icanread.com
Library of Congress Control Number: 2018938262
ISBN 978-0-06-235322-1 (trade bdg.)—ISBN 978-0-06-235321-4 (pbk.)

Book design by Celeste Knudsen

19 20 21 22 23   SCP   10 9 8 7 6 5 4 3 2 1   ❖   First Edition

DUCK, DUCK, DINOSAUR

SPRING SMILES

by Kallie George
Illustrated by Oriol Vidal

HARPER

An Imprint of HarperCollinsPublishers

This is Feather.
This is Flap.

And this is their brother, Spike.

It is spring.
Everyone smiles.

And the sun smiles back.
Time to explore.

"Look! A garden!" says Feather.
"Let's smell the flowers!"

"Flowers! Flowers!" says Flap.

"FLOWERS!" says Spike.

They smell the flowers.

Feather smiles.

Flap smiles.

Spike . . .

Sneezes!

ACHOOO!
Oh, no!

"Look! Leaves!" says Feather.
"Let's make hats!"
"Hats! Hats!" says Flap.

14

"HATS!" says Spike.

15

They make hats.

Feather smiles.

Flap smiles.

Spike . . .

Sneezes!

ACHOO!
Oh, no!

19

"Look! Seeds!" says Feather.
"Let's make a wish!"
"A wish! A wish!" says Flap.

"WISH!" says Spike.

21

They blow the wish.

Feather smiles.

Flap smiles.

Spike . . .

Sneezes!

24

ACHOO!
Oh, no!

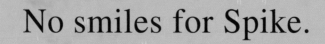

No smiles for Spike.

26

Drip, drip, drip.

"Look! Rain!" says Feather.
"Let's jump in puddles!"

"Puddles! Puddles!" says Flap.

"PUDDLES . . . ?" says Spike.

He is worried.

Will he sneeze?

Splish, splish, splish.
They jump in puddles.

Feather smiles.

Flap smiles.

And Spike . . .

. . . SMILES, too!

And a rainbow smiles back.